Mouse Cookies & More

Mouse Cookies
& More
A Treasury

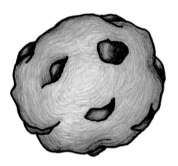

BY
Laura Numeroff

ILLUSTRATED BY
Felicia Bond

Laura Geringer Books
An Imprint of HarperCollinsPublishers

Mouse Cookies & More: A Treasury

Text copyright © 1985, 1991, 1998, 2002, 2006 by Laura Numeroff

Illustrations copyright © 1985, 1991, 1995, 1998, 2000, 2002, 2005, 2006 by Felicia Bond

Songs written by Sarah Weeks, ℗ 1993, 1994, 1997, 1999 by HarperCollins Publishers

Some recipes previously published in *Mouse Cookies: 10 Easy-to-Make Cookie Recipes* © 1995 by Felicia Bond and Laura Numeroff

PEANUTS © United Feature Syndicate, Inc.

Printed in the United States of America

www.harpercollinschildrens.com

Library of Congress Cataloging-in-Publication Data is available.

ISBN-10: 0-06-113763-4 — ISBN-13: 978-0-06-113763-1

14 15 16 CG/RRDC 20 ❖ First Edition

is a registered trademark of HarperCollins Publishers

When cooking, it is important to keep safety in mind. Children should always ask permission from an adult before cooking and should be supervised by an adult in the kitchen at all times. The publisher and authors disclaim any liability from any injury that might result from the use, proper or improper, of the recipes and activities contained in this book.

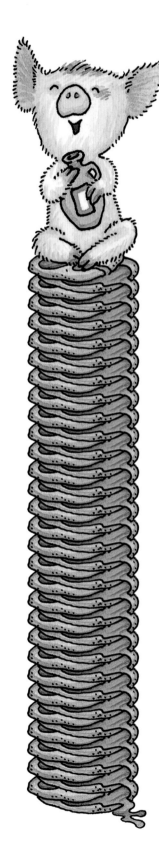

In memory of my mother and father

—L.N.

Special thanks, all these many years, to John Vitale

—F.B.

Table of Contents

*T*his book is especially for families, because family is very important to me. I grew up as the youngest of three girls. When I was little, my sisters and I used to play lots of games together. We loved to sing songs in the car on family trips too. At home, we always talked about our days around the dinner table with our parents. And I especially loved going to the museum with my dad.

When I was about nine years old, I started writing stories and drawing pictures to go with them. My three favorite possessions were my microscope, my box of sixty-four crayons, and my library card. While you read through this treasury, you'll be able to do science experiments, draw pictures, and read stories, just like I did when I was younger—and still do now! Well, maybe not the science experiments. . . .

I've been writing books about Mouse, Moose, and Pig for over twenty years, and in all that time they've started to feel like another kind of family. I also have some pets that are family to me. I have an Australian Shepherd named Sydney, and a cat named Petunia, but I call her Tuna for short. There are two cookie recipes in this treasury named in honor of Sydney and Tuna.

I hope you enjoy!

Love,

Laura Numeroff

When I was a little 👧 I loved to draw. I drew 🐴🐐🐄, 🏠🏘, Snoopy 🐶 and Lucy. I also loved to 📖. I rode my 🚲 to the library every week.

That was in New York. I grew up with four 👦👦👦👦 and two 👧👧. We had many pets. Today I still love all animals.

There are little things I put into my art that are parts of my life. The 👦 in IF YOU GIVE A 🐭 A 🍪 is my old boyfriend. It looks just like him, except now he has a 🧔. The 👧 in IF YOU GIVE A 🐷 A 🥞 is me. Too bad I never had a little pig; that would have been really cool.

I do many sketches to get my art just right. When things look the way I want them to I use 🖌 to paint them. Sometimes I add 🖊.

I have combined my love of art with my love of books.

I am happy. 👩 *Felicia Bond*

From the desk of Mouse

Mouse has many pairs of boxer shorts: polka dots, candy cane, and plaid.

—

If You Give a Mouse a Cookie

If You Give a

Mouse a Cookie

Laura Joffe Numeroff
ILLUSTRATED BY Felicia Bond

A Laura Geringer Book
An Imprint of HarperCollinsPublishers

For Florence & William Numeroff,
the two best parents anyone could
ever possibly want!   L. J. N.

For Stephen   F. B.

is a registered trademark of HarperCollins Publishers

If You Give a Mouse a Cookie
Text copyright © 1985 by Laura Joffe Numeroff
Illustrations copyright © 1985 by Felicia Bond
Library of Congress Cataloging in Publication Data
Numeroff, Laura Joffe.
   If you give a mouse a cookie.
   Summary: Relating the cycle of requests a mouse is likely to make
after you give him a cookie takes the reader through a young boy's
day.
   1. Children's stories, American. [1. Mice—Fiction]
I. Bond, Felicia, ill.   II. Title.
PZ7.N964If 1985   [E]   84-48343
ISBN-10: 0-06-024586-7 — ISBN-10: 0-06-024587-5 (lib. bdg.)
ISBN-13: 978-0-06-024586-3 — ISBN-13: 978-0-06-024587-0 (lib. bdg.)

If you give a mouse a cookie,

he's going to ask for a glass of milk.

When you give him the milk,

he'll probably ask you for a straw.

When he's finished, he'll ask for a napkin.

Then he'll want to look in a mirror
to make sure he doesn't
have a milk mustache.

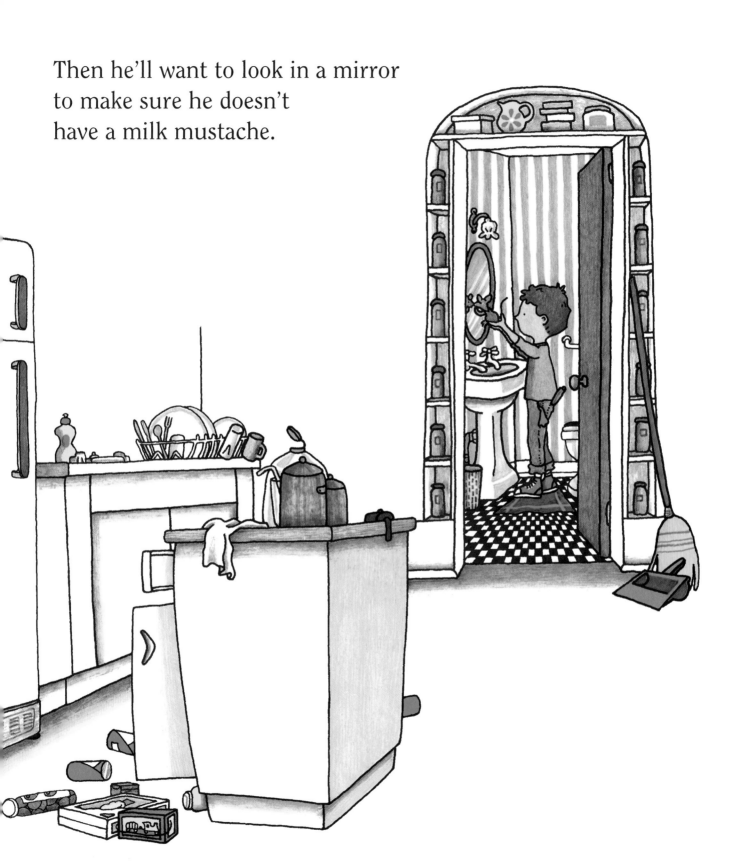

When he looks into the mirror,

he might notice his hair needs a trim.

So he'll probably ask
for a pair of nail scissors.

When he's finished giving himself a trim,
he'll want a broom to sweep up.

He'll start sweeping.

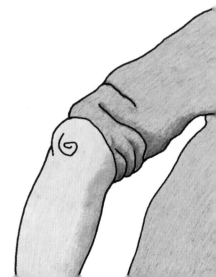

He might get carried away and sweep every room in the house.

He may even end up washing the floors as well!

When he's done,
    he'll probably want to take a nap.

You'll have to fix up a little box for him
with a blanket and a pillow.

He'll crawl in,
make himself comfortable
and fluff the pillow a few times.

He'll probably ask you to read him a story.

So you'll read to him from one of your books,
and he'll ask to see the pictures.

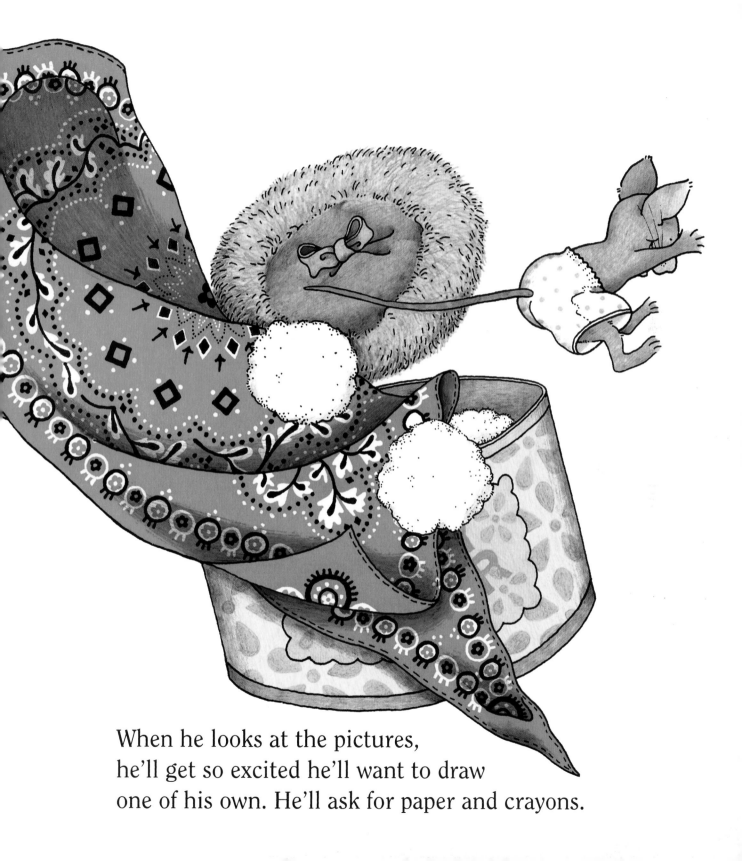

When he looks at the pictures,
he'll get so excited he'll want to draw
one of his own. He'll ask for paper and crayons.

He'll draw a picture.

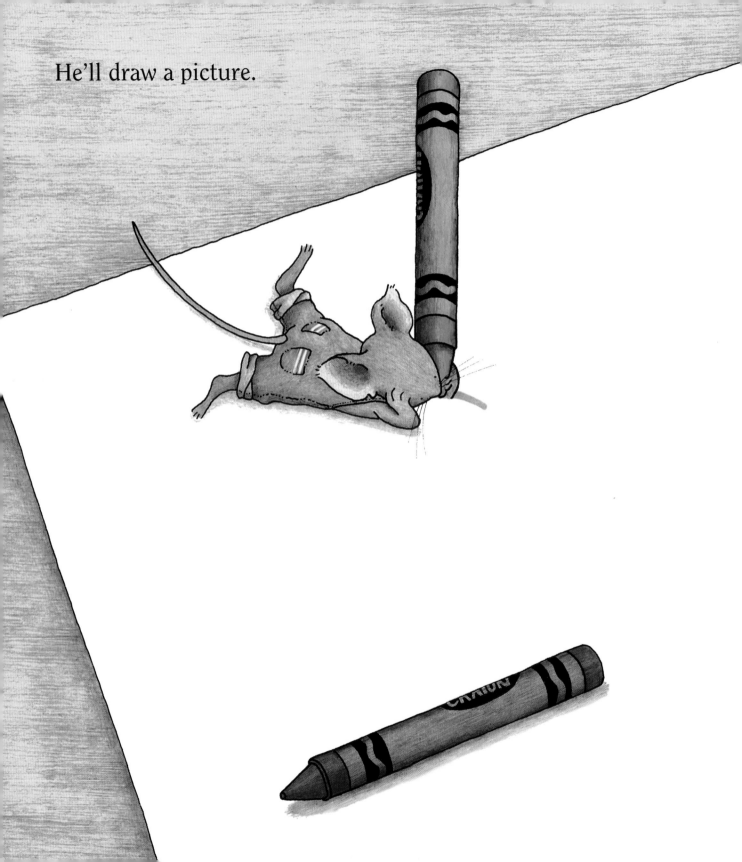

When the picture is finished,

he'll want to sign his name

with a pen.

Then he'll want to hang his picture on your refrigerator.

Which means he'll need

Scotch tape.

He'll hang up his drawing and stand back to look at it.

Looking at the refrigerator will remind him that

he's thirsty.

So . . .

he'll ask for a glass of milk.

And chances are if he asks for
a glass of milk,

he's going to want a cookie to go with it.

From the
desk of
Mouse

I came up with the idea
for this book when I was
on a long, boring car
trip!

—JW

From the
desk of
Mouse

I wrote the name of a friend in one
place in this book. It's in the large
drawing Mouse did of his family.

—JB

MOM'S
OLD-FASHIONED
OATMEAL COOKIES

36 cookies • 375°F oven

1 cup flour	**1 cup packed light brown sugar**
¼ teaspoon salt	**½ cup raisins**
1 teaspoon baking powder	**1 egg**
1 teaspoon cinnamon	**¼ cup vegetable oil**
1 cup rolled oats (not instant)	**¼ cup heavy cream**
½ teaspoon ginger	

1. Combine flour, salt, baking powder, cinnamon, oats, ginger, brown sugar, and raisins together in a bowl. Mix with your fingers, breaking up any lumps of brown sugar.

2. Using a spoon, stir in egg, vegetable oil, and cream. The batter will be hard to stir, but keep going until it is brown and gooey.

3. Drop batter by teaspoon onto a greased cookie sheet. Bake for 10–12 minutes.

UNCLE SYDNEY'S
SNICKERDOODLES

30 cookies • 375°F oven

1⅔ cups flour

½ teaspoon baking soda

½ teaspoon salt

½ teaspoon nutmeg

½ cup softened butter

¾ cup sugar

2 eggs

1 teaspoon vanilla extract

½ cup chopped walnuts

½ cup raisins

1 tablespoon cinnamon

¼ cup sugar

1. Combine flour, baking soda, salt, and nutmeg. Set aside.

2. In a bowl, mash butter and sugar together until well blended. Add eggs and vanilla, and mix until light and fluffy. Add the flour mixture, and stir until well combined. Stir in walnuts and raisins.

3. Mix cinnamon and sugar on plate. Roll pieces of the dough into one-inch balls. Roll each ball in the cinnamon-sugar mixture, and place on a greased cookie sheet. Bake for 10–12 minutes.

POP'S
PEANUT BUTTER MUNCHES

30 cookies • 350°F oven

1 cup peanut butter (creamy or crunchy)
1 cup sugar
1 egg

1. Combine all ingredients in a bowl. Mix well.

2. Using your hands, roll the dough into one-inch balls and drop onto a lightly greased cookie sheet.

3. Bake for 10–12 minutes until golden brown. Press the tines of a fork into each cookie while still soft.

The Mouse Cookie

by Sarah Weeks

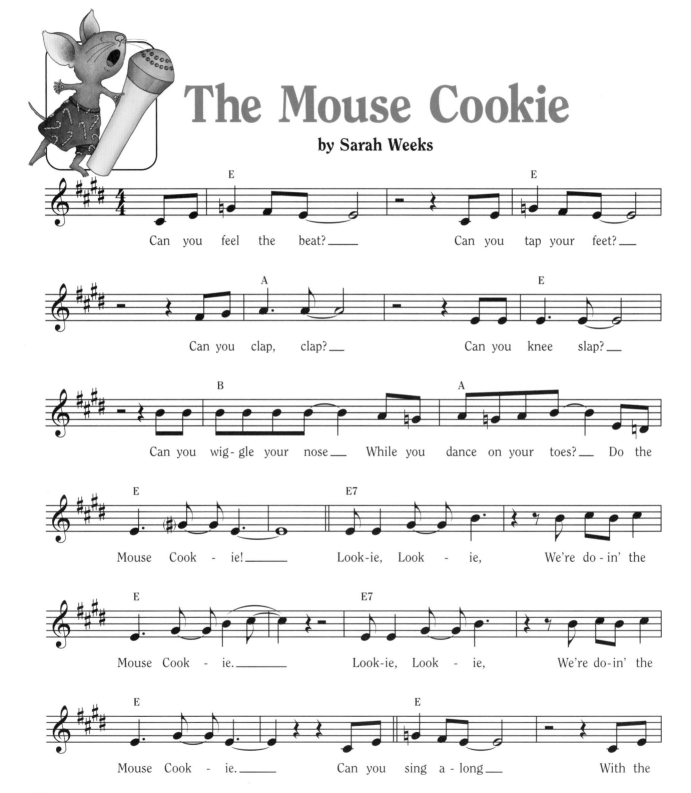

Can you feel the beat?____ Can you tap your feet?__

Can you clap, clap?__ Can you knee slap?__

Can you wig-gle your nose__ While you dance on your toes?__ Do the

Mouse Cook - ie!_____ Look-ie, Look - ie, We're do-in' the

Mouse Cook - ie._____ Look-ie, Look - ie, We're do-in' the

Mouse Cook - ie._____ Can you sing a-long__ With the

cook - ie song? __ Can you hip - hop? __ Can you

be - bop? __ Can you wig - gle your nose __ While you

dance on your toes? __ Do the Mouse Cook - ie. _____

Ev - 'ry - bod - y's do - ing it, It's eas - y as pie, _____

All you do is wig - gle, Won't you give it a try? __

Get up on your tip - py toes, Now don't be shy, __ If __

__ you do the Cook - ie, ba - by, so will I. _____

Look - ie, Look - ie, We're do - in' the Mouse Cook - ie._____

Look - ie, Look - ie, We're do - in' the Mouse Cook - ie._____

_____ Once you get it right, ___ You can

dance all night, ___ You can jump jump, ___ You can

bump bump, You can wig - gle your nose ___ While you

dance on your toes, ___ Do the Mouse Cook - ie! ___

Ev - 'ry - bod - y's do - ing it, It's eas - y as pie, _____

All you do is wig - gle, Won't you give it a try? ___

Get up on your tip - py toes, Now don't be shy, ___ If ___

___ you do the Cook - ie, ba - by, so will I. ___

repeat to fade

Look-ie, Look - ie, We're do-in' the Mouse Cook - ie. ___

Look - ie, Look - ie, We're do-in' the Mouse Cook - ie. ___

Wrong Words

by Sarah Weeks

No... You'll get a lit-tle pair of scis-sors for him. *Right!* It's

gon-na make a mess, Which you'll clean up more or less. He'll be

tir-ed and he'll want to take a bus. *No...* He'll be tir-ed and he'll want to take a

nap! *Right!* So you'll fix up a box With a blan-ket and a fox.

No... A blan-ket and a pil-low. *Right!* And he'll climb right

in! He'll fluff up the chick-en. *No.* He'll fluff up the piz-za. *No.* He'll

fluff up the pil-low. *Right!* And he'll say to you:

Please won't you read me the men-u? *No.* Please won't you read me a sto-ry?

Right. So you read __ to him from one of your books, And he'll

ask to see ___ the pic - tures, But when he looks at __

__ the pic - tures, He'll want to draw one of his own, ___

So he'll ask for some tooth - paste. *No...* He'll ask for some pap - er.

Right. And a box of cray-ons And he'll draw a pic - ture. *instrumental*

When the pic-ture's done, He'll sign his lit - tle name, And he'll

58

Draw Your Own Family Portrait

In *If You Give a Mouse a Cookie*, Mouse draws a picture of his whole family. He even draws his house! Then he hangs it on the refrigerator. Mouse loves drawing.

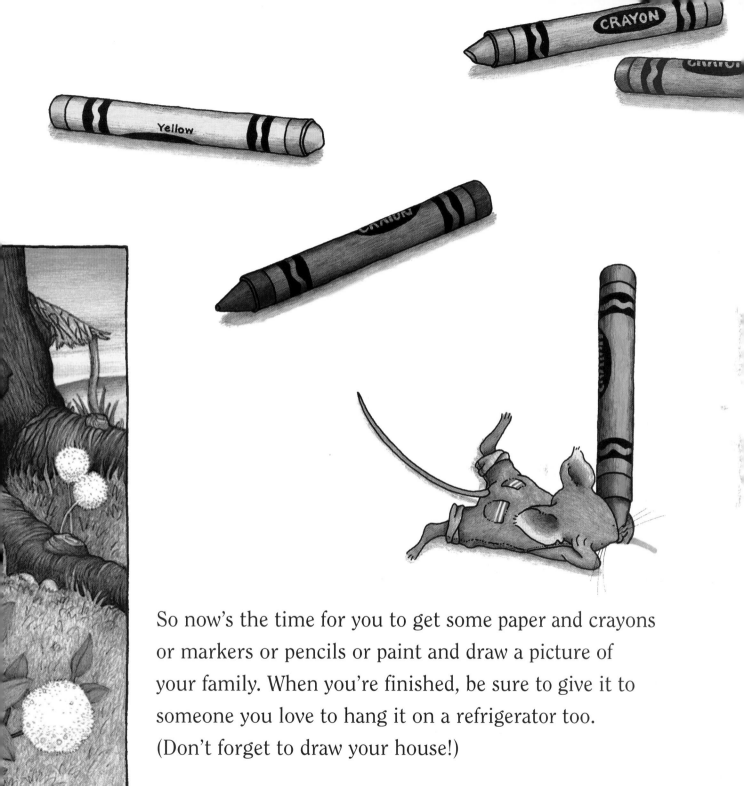

So now's the time for you to get some paper and crayons or markers or pencils or paint and draw a picture of your family. When you're finished, be sure to give it to someone you love to hang it on a refrigerator too. (Don't forget to draw your house!)

Find the Real Mouse

Take a good look at the Mouse on this page. Do you see how long his tail is? Do you see what his ears look like? Check out his overalls. . . . Now look at the Mouse pictures on the next page. Can you tell which one is the real Mouse?

A

B

C

D

E

F

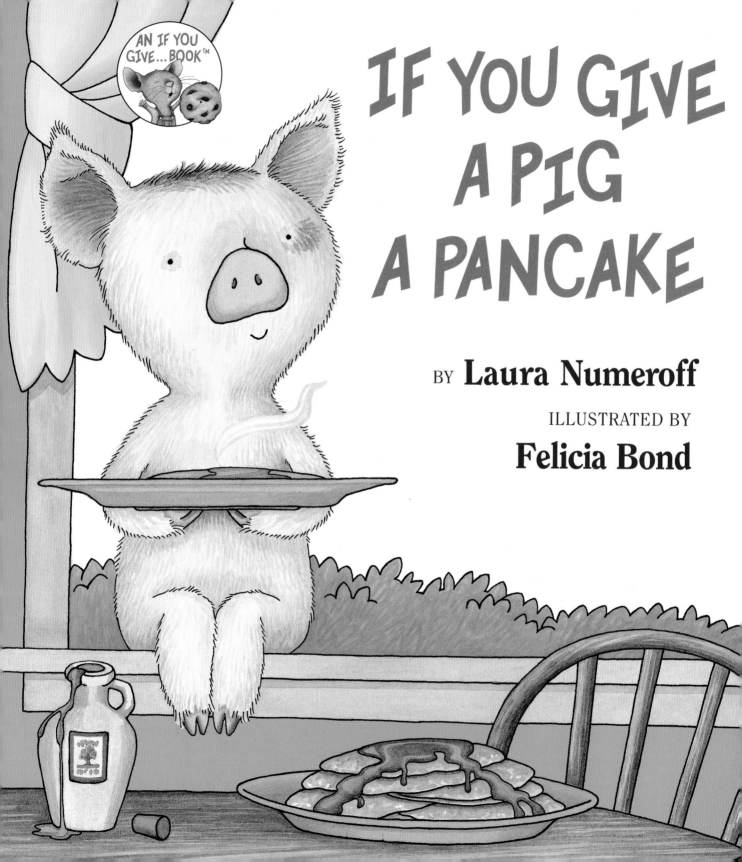

AN IF YOU
GIVE...BOOK™

IF YOU GIVE
A PIG
A PANCAKE

BY **Laura Numeroff**

ILLUSTRATED BY
Felicia Bond

If You Give a Pig a Pancake

Once again, for Stephen —F.B.
For Laura Geringer, with love and eternal gratitude —L.N.

If You Give a

If You Give a Pig a Pancake
Text copyright © 1998 by Laura Numeroff
Illustrations copyright © 1998 by Felicia Bond
Printed in the U.S.A. All rights reserved.
www.harperchildrens.com

Library of Congress Cataloging-in-Publication Data
Numeroff, Laura Joffe.
   If you give a pig a pancake / by Laura Numeroff ; illustrated by Felicia Bond.
      p.   cm.
"A Laura Geringer Book"
   Summary: One thing leads to another when you give a pig a pancake.
   ISBN 0-06-026686-4. — ISBN 0-06-026687-2 (lib. bdg.)
   [1. Pigs—Fiction.]   I. Bond, Felicia, ill.   II. Title.
PZ7.N964Ih   1998   97-36832
[E]—DC21   CIP
                                                                AC

Pig a Pancake

BY **Laura Numeroff**

ILLUSTRATED BY **Felicia Bond**

A Laura Geringer Book
An Imprint of HarperCollins*Publishers*

If you give a pig a pancake,

she'll want some syrup to go with it.

You'll give her some of your favorite maple syrup.

She'll probably get all sticky,

so she'll want to take a bath.

She'll ask you for
some bubbles.

When you give her the bubbles,
she'll probably ask you for a toy.
You'll have to find your rubber duck.

The duck will remind her of the farm where she was born. She might feel homesick and want to visit her family.

She'll want you to come too.
She'll look through your closet
for a suitcase.

Then she'll look under your bed.

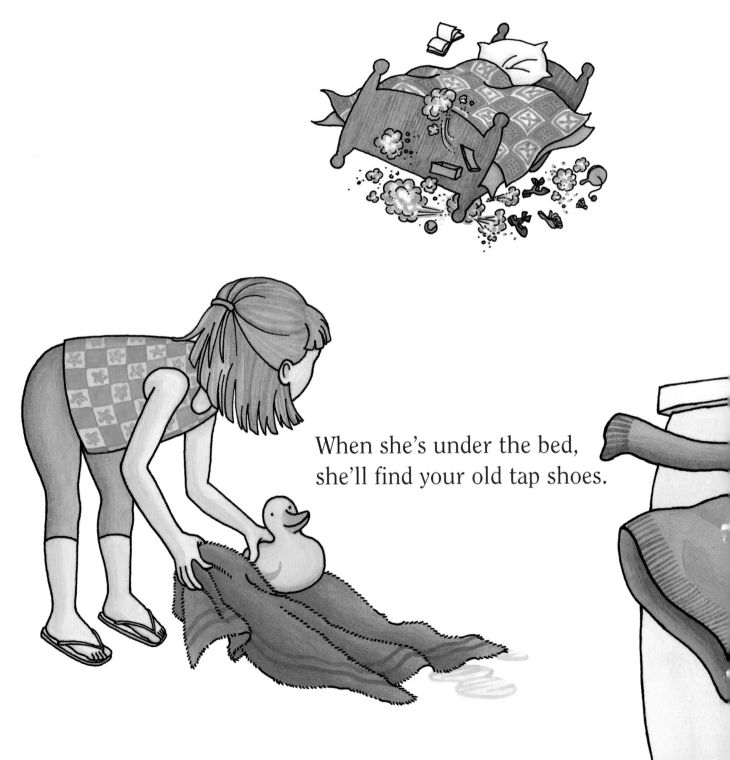

When she's under the bed,
she'll find your old tap shoes.

She'll try them on. She'll probably
need something special to
wear with them.

When she's all dressed, she'll ask for some music.

You'll play your
very best piano piece,
and she'll start dancing.

Then she'll want you to take her picture.

So you'll have to get your camera.

When she sees the picture,

she'll ask you to take more.

Then she'll want to send one to each of her friends.

You'll have to give her
some envelopes and stamps

and take her to the mailbox.

On the way, she'll see the tree in your backyard.
She'll want to build a tree house.

So you'll have to get her some wood,
a hammer, and some nails.

When the tree house is finished,

she'll want to decorate it.

She'll ask for wallpaper and glue.

When she hangs the wallpaper, she'll get all sticky.

Feeling sticky will remind her of your favorite maple syrup.

She'll probably ask you for some.

And chances are,

if she asks you for some syrup,

she'll want a pancake to go with it.

From the
desk of
Pig

I loved taking tap-dancing
lessons when I was a little
girl even though I wasn't
very good.

—JW

From the
desk of
Pig

My cats lie on my drawing table
while I work. They push things off
the edge, which they find very
funny. It takes me six months to
illustrate a book.

—JB

Tips

 **MIXING:**

- Never overmix. Beat just until combined, ignoring a few lumps.
- For thinner pancakes, add a little water.
- After mixing, batter can be refrigerated for up to six hours.

 **PANS:**

- Cast-iron and nonstick skillets and griddles don't need oiling or greasing. Others do. If you need to add oil or butter, do it between batches.
- The pan is hot enough for the batter when a few drops of water bounce on the surface of the skillet.

 POURING:

- When pouring batter into the pan, leave a little room between pancakes.
- For nice, round pancakes, pour the batter from close to the pan.

 FLIPPING:

- Pancakes should be flipped when the top begins bubbling and the under-side is lightly browned.
- Flip only once, and remove when second side is cooked.

 EATING:

- Pancakes are best served immediately, but to serve together keep them warm by placing them on an oven-proof platter in a 180–200°F oven after you cook them.

PANCAKE PARTY BOWL
with BERRIES AND CREAM

1 large pancake • 375°F oven

1 cup flour

1 tablespoon sugar

1¼ cups milk

2 eggs

¼ teaspoon salt

4 cups mixed fresh fruit
   (or 2 12-ounce bags mixed
   frozen fruit, defrosted)

¼ cup sugar

1 tablespoon melted butter

3 tablespoons confectioner's sugar

whipped cream

1. Thoroughly butter a 9-inch pie plate.

2. Combine the flour, 1 tablespoon sugar, milk, eggs, and salt in a bowl and whisk until bubbly, about 1 minute. Pour the batter into the pie plate. Bake until the edges rise and the center is still soft.

3. While the pancake is cooking, toss the fruit and ¼ cup sugar in a bowl. When the pancake is finished, remove from the oven. Fill with the fruit. Sift confectioner's sugar over the top. Serve immediately with whipped cream.

103

ICE CREAM PANCAKES
with STRAWBERRY SAUCE

4 large pancakes

1 pint vanilla ice cream	**oil, as needed**
1 cup water	
1 egg	**Strawberry Sauce**
1 cup flour	**1 pint fresh or defrosted**
1½ teaspoons baking powder	**strawberries, sliced**
pinch salt	**¼ cup sugar**

1. Combine 1 cup ice cream with the water and egg in a bowl. Mix thoroughly. In a separate bowl, blend together flour, baking powder, and salt. Add the wet mixture to the dry mixture and stir until combined. Do not overmix.

2. Heat a lightly greased skillet over medium heat. Drop about ⅓ cup of batter onto the skillet for each pancake. After about 1 minute, when the pancakes start to bubble and are lightly browned on the bottom, flip them. Cook on the other side, just until lightly browned.

3. Toss strawberries and sugar together in a bowl. Let sit 15 minutes to 1 hour. Gently mash the berries with a potato masher.

4. Place 1 pancake in the center of each plate. Top with a small scoop of ice cream. Divide the fresh Strawberry Sauce among the pancakes. Serve immediately.

Flippin' the Flapjacks

Words by Sarah Weeks   Music by Michael Abbott

Some peo-ple call 'em pan___ cakes, Some peo-ple call 'em hot___ stacks,

Some peo-ple call 'em grid-dle cakes,___ Me? I call 'em flap-jacks. No

mat-ter what you call 'em,___ Here's a lit-tle tip,___ When they're

done on one___ side,___ All you got-ta do is... FLIP.___

Making pancakes is easy—you can even use a mix. The tricky part is flipping them over.
It takes a lot of practice. Why don't we practice right now?
Turn both of your hands palm up, and when I count to three, flip them over so your palms are facing the floor.
Ready? Palms up—one, two, three...FLIP. Very good!
Now...when you hear the flipping sound, flip your flapjacks along with me. OK?

Now that you're such expert flapjack flippers, let's try something a little more challenging.

107

Flip-pin' the flap - jacks, _____ Flip, flip, flip-pin' the flap - jacks.

Some peo-ple like 'em gold - en, Some peo-ple like 'em brown, _____

Some peo-ple pour on syr - up Un - til those flap - jacks drown, _____ No

mat-ter how you like 'em _____ Here's a lit-tle tip, _____ When they're

done on one _____ side, _____ All you got-ta do is... FLIP. _____

Flip 'em high, _ Flip 'em low, _____ Flip 'em fast, _____

108

Flip 'em slow, _ Flip 'em front, _ Flip 'em back, _

Now you're flip - pin' _ the flap - jack! _

Flip-pin' the flap - jacks, _____ Flip-pin' the flap - jacks, _____

Flip-pin' the flap - jacks, _ Flip, flip, flip-pin' the flap - jacks. *Yeah!*

The Piggy Polka

Words by Sarah Weeks   Music by Michael Abbott

This dance is ver - y sim - ple, I'll tell you what to do, We'll

start off ver - y slow - ly, And speed up when we're through. Step right, left,

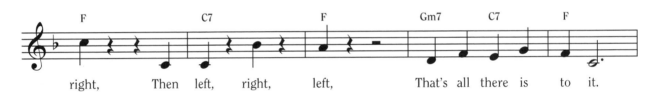

right, Then left, right, left, That's all there is to it.

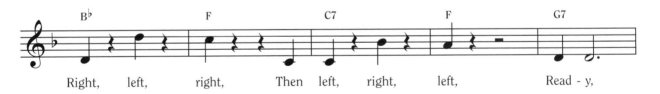

Right, left, right, Then left, right, left, Read - y,

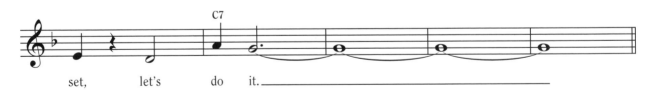

set, let's do it.

You don't have to have a tail, Fam - ous for its curl Or

110

lit - tle hooves that click - i - ty clack, Ev - 'ry time you twirl. You don't have to

have a snout, A sim - ple nose will do. Just grab your - self a part - ner, This

dance is made for two._____ Oh, do the Pig - gy Pol - ka

All a-round the room, If you don't have a part - ner, Try danc-ing with a broom. It's

called the Pig - gy Pol - ka, It's lots of fun to do, Now

choose an-oth - er part - ner And dance with some - one new._____ *Here we go!*

Right, left, right, Left, right, left. Right, left, right, Left, right, left.

111

Right, left, right, Left, right, left. Right, left, right, Left, right, left.

You don't have to roll in mud or walk on all four feet,

You don't have to oink a lot or eat and eat and eat.____ You don't have to

be a pig, You're fine the way you are, So clap your hands to - geth - er If you

like this dance so far._____ Oh,

do the Pig - gy Pol - ka All a - round the room, If you don't have a

part - ner, Try danc - ing with a broom. It's called the Pig - gy Pol - ka, It's

lots of fun to do, Now choose an-oth-er part-ner And

dance with some-one new._____ *Here we go!* Right, left, right, Left, right, left.

Right, left, right, Left, right, left. Right, left, right,

Left, right, left. Right, left, right, Left, right, left.

Right, left, right, Left, right, left. Right, left, right,

Left, right, left. Right, left, right, Left, right, left.

Right, left, right, Left, right, left.

Write Your Friend a Letter

In *If You Give a Pig a Pancake*, Pig mails pictures to her friends. If you don't have pictures handy, you can send your friends letters instead. Here's a letter that you can copy, fill-in-the-blanks, and mail. Be sure to ask a grown-up to help you address the envelope and to get you a stamp.

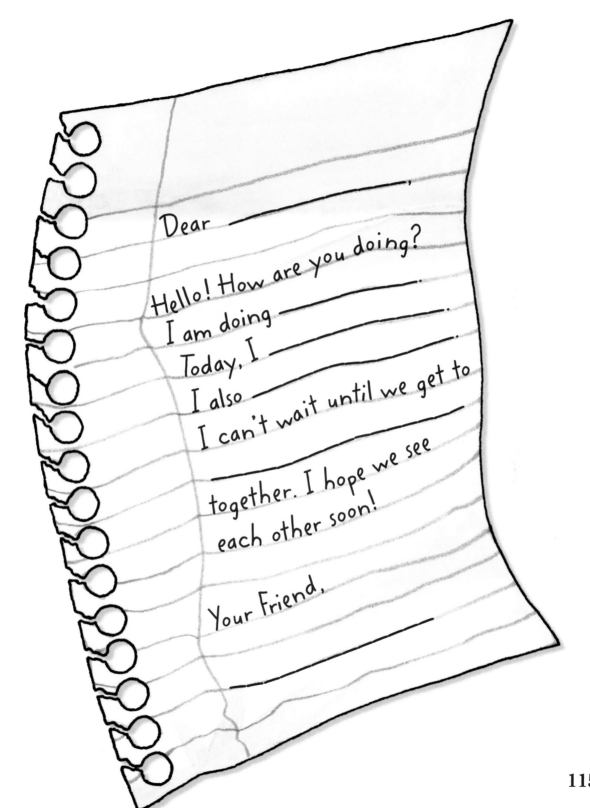

115

Where's Pig?

Pig is hiding in a messy closet. Can you find her? What about her tap shoes? Can you find the letter she wrote to her friend? And what about her hairbrush? There's also a bottle of syrup here, if you look hard enough. . . .

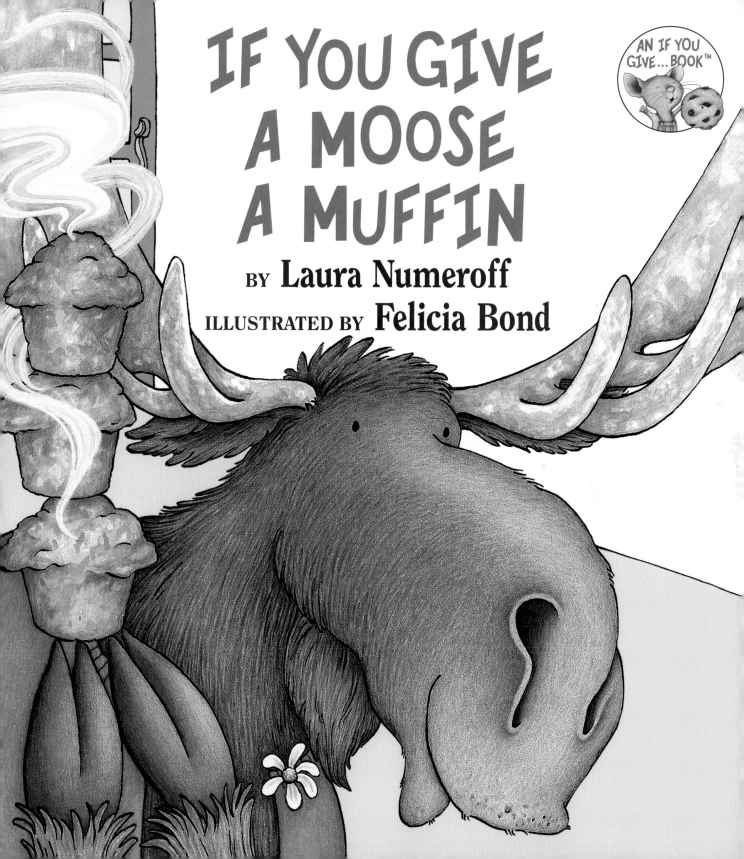

IF YOU GIVE A MOOSE A MUFFIN

BY **Laura Numeroff**

ILLUSTRATED BY **Felicia Bond**

AN IF YOU GIVE... BOOK™

IF YOU GIVE A
MOOSE A MUFFIN

by Laura Joffe Numeroff

illustrated by Felicia Bond

A Laura Geringer Book

An Imprint of HarperCollinsPublishers

If You Give a Moose a Muffin
Text copyright © 1991 by Laura Numeroff
Illustrations copyright © 1991 by Felicia Bond
Printed in the U.S.A. All rights reserved.

Library of Congress Cataloging-in-Publication Data

Numeroff, Laura Joffe.
   If you give a moose a muffin / by Laura Joffe Numeroff ;
illustrated by Felicia Bond.
      p.   cm.
   "A Laura Geringer book."
   Summary: Chaos can ensue if you give a moose a muffin and start
him on a cycle of urgent requests.
   ISBN 0-06-024405-4. — ISBN 0-06-024406-2 (lib. bdg.)
   [1. Moose—Fiction.]   I. Bond, Felicia, ill.   II. Title.
PZ7.N964Id   1991   91-2207
[E]—dc20   CIP
                                                                AC

is a registered trademark of HarperCollins Publishers

For Alice and Emily, the two best sisters
anyone could ever possibly want!
L.J.N.

For Antoine, Nahem, Jennifer, Santos, Brian and Crystal
F.B.

If you give a moose a muffin,

he'll want some jam to go with it.

So you'll bring out some of your mother's homemade blackberry jam.

When he's finished eating
the muffin, he'll want another.

And another.

And another.
When they're all gone,
he'll ask you to make more.

You'll have to go to the store to get some muffin mix.

He'll want to go with you.

When he opens the door and feels how chilly it is, he'll ask to borrow a sweater.

When he puts the sweater on,
he'll notice one of the buttons
is loose.

He'll ask for a needle and thread.

He'll start sewing.
The button will remind him of the
puppets his grandmother
used to make.

So he'll ask for some old socks.

He'll make sock puppets.

When they're done, he'll want to put on a puppet show.

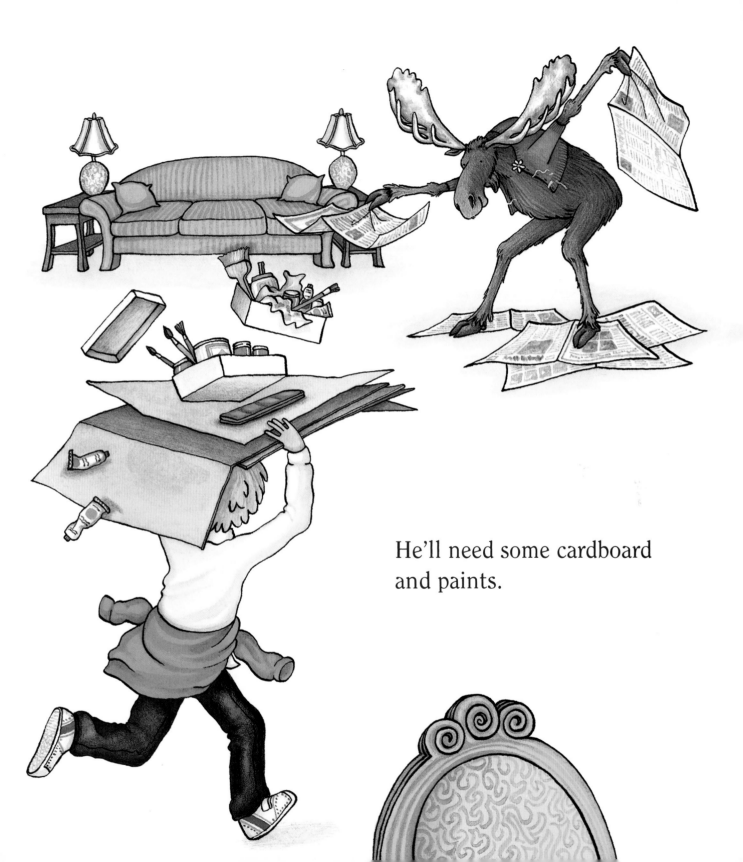

He'll need some cardboard
and paints.

Then he'll ask you to help make the scenery.

When the scenery is finished, he'll get behind the couch.
But his antlers will stick out.

So he'll ask for something to cover them up.

You'll bring him a sheet from your bed.

When he sees the sheet, he'll remember
he wants to be a ghost for Halloween.

He'll try it on and shout,

"BOO!"

It'll scare him
so much, he'll knock
over the paints.

So he'll use the sheet
to clean up the mess.

Then he'll ask for some soap to wash it out.

He'll probably want to hang the sheet up to dry.

He'll go outside to put it
on the clothesline.

When he's out in the yard, he'll see
your mother's blackberry bushes.

Seeing the blackberries
will remind him of
her jam.

He'll probably ask you for some.

And chances are . . .

if you give him the jam,

he'll want a muffin to go with it.

From the
desk of
Moose

When I illustrated this book I had three cats, named Otis, Pro, and Mickey. I wrote their names on the pages where Moose is painting.

—JHS

 From the
desk of
Moose

I've never seen a real live moose, but I'm hoping to someday!

—JW

154

CORNY CORN MUFFINS

12 muffins • 400°F oven

4 cups flour
2 cups cornmeal
4 tablespoons sugar
2 teaspoons baking powder
1½ teaspoons salt
3 eggs
¾ cup vegetable oil
1 8.5-ounce can cream-style corn

1. Make sure rack is in center of oven. Generously spray or grease muffin cups and the top of a tin.

2. In a large bowl, with a whisk or fork, combine the flour, cornmeal, sugar, baking powder, and salt. In a medium bowl, mix the eggs with a fork, then stir in the vegetable oil and creamed corn. Stir the wet mixture into the dry mixture just until combined.

3. With wet hands, roll batter into loosely formed balls about the size of each muffin cup, dropping each into a cup as you work. Bake muffins for about 20–25 minutes or until a toothpick inserted into the center comes out clean or with a few dry crumbs.

155

CHOCOLATE MUD MUFFINS

12 muffins • 400°F oven

2 cups flour	1¼ teaspoons baking	¼ cup vegetable oil
1¼ cups sugar	soda	2 teaspoons vanilla
⅓ cup cocoa	½ teaspoon salt	
1 teaspoon cinnamon	1¼ cups buttermilk	

Moose Treats — Choose 1 or more of these to *total* one cup:
chocolate chips
colored chocolate-covered peanuts
chocolate-covered peanut-butter pieces

1. Make sure rack is in center of oven. Generously spray or grease muffin cups and the top of a tin.

2. In a large bowl, with a fork or whisk, combine the flour, sugar, cocoa, baking soda, cinnamon, and salt. In a medium bowl, mix buttermilk, oil, and vanilla. Add the wet mixture to the dry mixture, then stir just until combined. In 2 or 3 strokes, mix in moose treats. (Optional: hold back about ¼ cup of treats to sprinkle on top.)

3. Divide the "mud" equally among muffin cups, then sprinkle the remaining treats on top, if you wish. (You can taste the batter — no eggs!) Bake about 25–30 minutes or until the tops are very well cooked.

Making Muffins

by Sarah Weeks

Wan- na make muf-fins, A spe-cial way,__ Just do what I do,__ And

say what I say.__ Read-y? (Read-y!) Scoop, scoop,

in goes the flo - ur. (Scoop, scoop, in goes the flo - ur.) Crack, crack

in go the eggs. (Crack, crack in go the eggs.) Sprin - kle,__

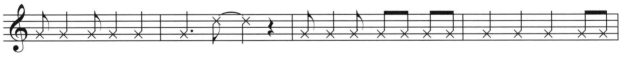

in goes the su - gar. (Sprin - kle,__ in goes the su-gar.) And a splash of milk. (And a

splash of milk.) And a pinch of salt. (And a pinch of salt.)

Uh oh, we forgot to pick the berries! Better hurry outside to the berry bush!

Zip,   zip,   zip on your jack - et.   (Zip,   zip,   zip on   your   jack - et.)

Slip,   slip,   slip on your boots.   (Slip,   slip,   slip on   your   boots.)

Run,   run   out to   the bush.   (Run,   run   out to   the bush.)

Pick,   pick,   pick,   pick.   (Pick,   pick,   pick,   pick.)   Scoot,   scoot   back

_ to   the house.   (Scoot,   scoot   back _ to   the house.)   Zip off   your jack - et.

(Zip off   your jack - et.)   Slip   off   your boots.   (Slip   off   your boots.)   Now...

Plip, plop, drop in the ber - ries. (Plip, plop, drop in the ber - ries.)

Stir it up, stir it up, stir it up. __ (Stir it up, stir it up, stir it up.) __

Drip, drop, pour in the bat - ter. (Drip, drop, pour in the bat - ter.) __

Put 'em in the ov - en. (Put 'em in the ov - en.) Tick - tock,

set the tim - er. (Tick - tock, set the tim - er.) And wait. (And

wait.) And wait. (And wait.) Ding! Ding! Read-y! (Ding! Ding!

Read - y!) Puff, puff, cool them off. __ (Puff, puff,

160

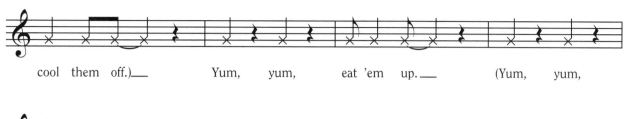

cool them off.)___ Yum, yum, eat 'em up.___ (Yum, yum,

eat 'em up.)___ Ah... muf-fins. (Ah... muf-fins.)

161

Doin' the Moose

by Sarah Weeks

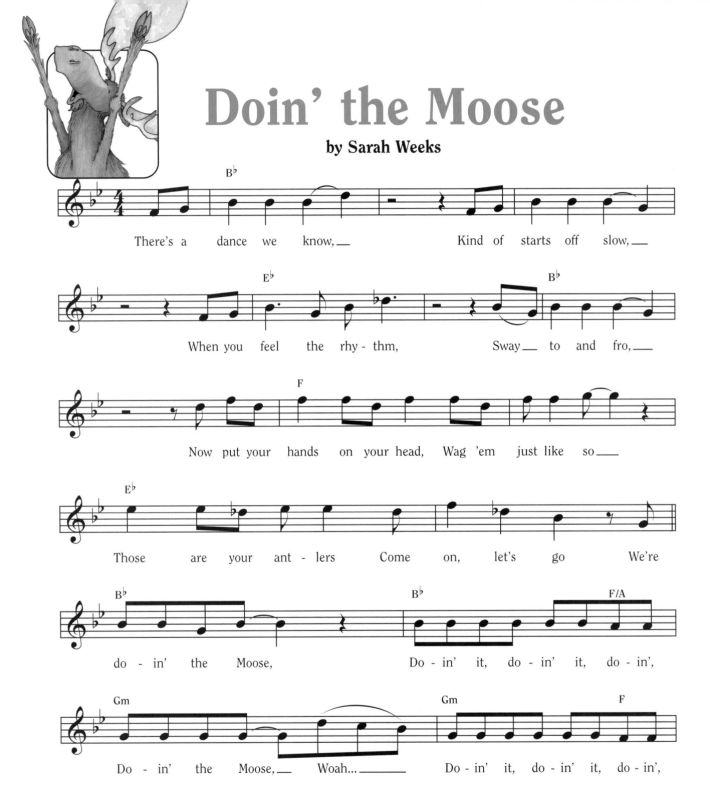

There's a dance we know, — Kind of starts off slow, —

When you feel the rhy - thm, Sway — to and fro, —

Now put your hands on your head, Wag 'em just like so —

Those are your ant - lers Come on, let's go We're

do - in' the Moose, Do - in' it, do - in' it, do - in',

Do - in' the Moose, — Woah... Do - in' it, do - in' it, do - in',

Do-in' the Moose, Oh, yeah We're do-in' the Moose.___

Can you stamp your hooves, To these hap-'nin' grooves,

I tell ya this dance proves,___ Who's got the

moos-i-est moves.___ Oh, you may be tired,___ a-

huf-fin' and puf-fin', Don't stop now to have___

___ a muf-fin! 'Cause we're do-in' the Moose,

Do-in' it, do-in' it, do-in', Do-in' the Moose,___ Whoa...___

163

Do - in' it, do - in' it, do - in', Do - in' the Moose, Oh,

yeah, We're do - in' the Moose.___ Out on the play-ground, In

back of the school, Ev - 'ry - bod - y's danc - ing like a cra - zy fool,___

Ant - lers in the air, Hooves cut - ting loose Look out, ev - 'ry - bod - y, We're

do - in' the Moose.___ *instrumental* Drums kick the beat, Sax - o - phone wails,

Ev - 'ry - bod - y shak - ing those___ moose tails,___ Fur be - gins to fly,

Turn - in' on the juice, Look out, world,___ We're do - in' the Moose!___

Make Your Own Sock Puppets

In *If You Give a Moose a Muffin,* Moose makes sock puppets. Then he puts on a puppet show. You can be just like Moose and make sock puppets of your own. Here's how:

First, get some old socks—make sure to ask permission before turning a sock into a puppet!

Next, get some markers. If you want to be fancy, you can get glue, buttons, extra fabric, and scissors too.

Put your hand in your sock so that four of your fingers are in the toe part of the sock and your thumb is in the heel part. When you move your hand, it will look like your sock puppet is opening its mouth.

Now you can decorate your puppet—give it eyes, a tongue, ears, a nose—anything you want!

Once you have a whole bunch of sock puppets, you can put on a puppet show for your family and friends, just like Moose does.

Moose's Word Search

Can you find these words?

Moose	Boy	Puppet	Newspaper
Muffins	Blackberry	Paint	Mess
Jam	Bush	Sock	Sweater

Q W A S Z X E R B O Y
D S W E A T E R L F C
M O O S E V T J A M Y
U C P U P P E T C E G
F K H P A I N T K S B
F N U B I J K M B S O
I P L U L A N J E L M
N E W S P A P E R I K
S T E H G R E S R N E
A L S U T B E J Y O S

IF YOU TAKE A MOUSE TO SCHOOL

BY **Laura Numeroff**

ILLUSTRATED BY **Felicia Bond**

If You Take a Mouse to School

If You Take a

BY Laura Numeroff

ILLUSTRATED BY Felicia Bond

 Laura Geringer Books

An Imprint of HarperCollins*Publishers*

is a registered trademark of HarperCollins Publishers

If You Take a Mouse to School
Text copyright © 2002 by Laura Numeroff
Illustrations copyright © 2002 by Felicia Bond
Printed in the U.S.A. All rights reserved.
www.harperchildrens.com

Library of Congress Cataloging-in-Publication Data
Numeroff, Laura Joffe.
    If you take a mouse to school / by Laura Numeroff ; illustrated by Felicia Bond.
        p.   cm.
    Summary: Follows a boy and his mouse through a busy day at school.
    ISBN-10: 0-06-028328-9 — ISBN-10: 0-06-028329-7 (lib. bdg.)
    ISBN-13: 978-0-06-028328-5 — ISBN-13: 978-0-06-028329-2 (lib. bdg.)
    [1. Schools—Fiction.   2. Mice—Fiction.]   I. Bond, Felicia, ill.   II. Title.
PZ7.N964Ii   2002   00-067280
[E]—dc21   CIP
                                                                          AC

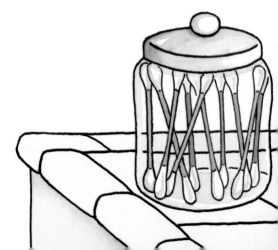

Mouse to School

If you take a mouse to school,

he'll ask you for your lunchbox.

When you give him your lunchbox,
he'll want a sandwich—

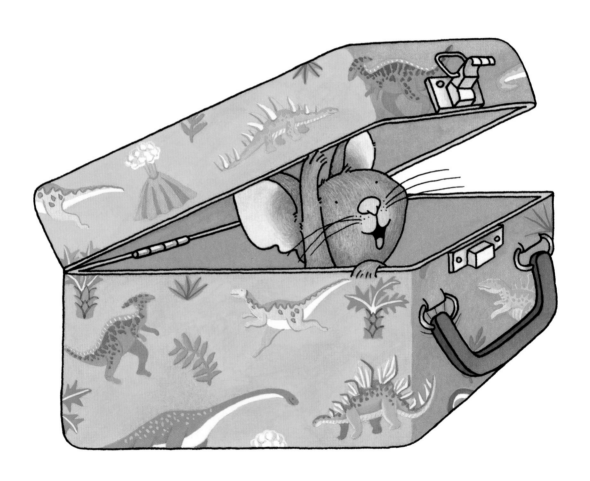

and a snack for later.
Then he'll need a notebook
and some pencils.

He'll probably want to share your backpack, too.

When you get to school,
he'll put his things
in your locker
and take a look around.

He might do a little math,

and spell a word or two.

He'll even try a science experiment!

Then he'll need to wash up.

You'll have to take him to the bathroom.

Once he's nice and clean,

he'll be ready for his lunch.

On the way to the lunchroom,
he'll see some building blocks.

He'll build a little mouse house

and make some furniture out of clay.

Then he'll need some books
for his bookshelf.
He'll start by writing
one of his own,
so he'll need a lot of paper.

He'll probably use up all
your pencils.

When he's finished,

he'll want to read his book to you.

Then he'll want to take it home.
So he'll put it in your lunchbox,

and tuck it in a safe place.

When the bell rings,
he'll run out to wait for the bus.

While he's waiting,
he'll play a quick game of soccer.

Then he'll ask you to
shoot a few baskets,

and do a little skateboarding.

When he stops to catch his breath,
he'll want to eat his snack.

So he'll ask you for your . . .

lunchbox.

And chances are,

if he asks you for your lunchbox,

you'll have to take him

back to school.

From the desk of **Mouse**

When I was six, my brother and I used to build houses out of blocks. We parked toy cars in the garage, just like Mouse does.

—JB

From the desk of **Mouse**

When I went to school, my favorite subject was science.

—JW

AUNT PETUNIA'S
JUMBO CHOCOLATE CHIP COOKIES

8 cookies • 350°F oven

1 cup plus 2 tablespoons flour
½ teaspoon baking soda
pinch salt
½ cup softened butter
1 teaspoon vanilla extract
½ cup sugar

¼ cup packed light brown sugar
1 egg
1 cup chocolate chips

1. Combine the flour, baking soda, and salt. Set aside.

2. In a bowl, mash together the butter, vanilla, sugar, and brown sugar until smooth and fluffy. Add the egg. Gradually add the flour mixture and mix until just blended. Stir in the chocolate chips, adding 1 teaspoon of water if necessary to help mix.

3. Grease two cookie sheets. Using your hands, place four big balls of dough on each sheet, spacing them evenly. Moisten your hands and press each piece of dough to flatten it out.
Bake for 12 minutes.

GRANDPA EDSEL'S
SUPER S'MORES

8 sandwiches • 350°F oven

8 graham crackers, broken in half
¾ cup mini marshmallows
3 tablespoons chocolate chips
16 thin banana slices (optional)

1. Set out 8 cracker halves on a baking sheet. Pack as many marshmallows and chips as you can fit onto each cracker. (Optional: top with two thin slices of banana.) Cover with the other cracker half to make 8 sandwiches.

2. Bake for 5 minutes or until chocolate and marshmallows are melted. Let stand until cool enough to eat.

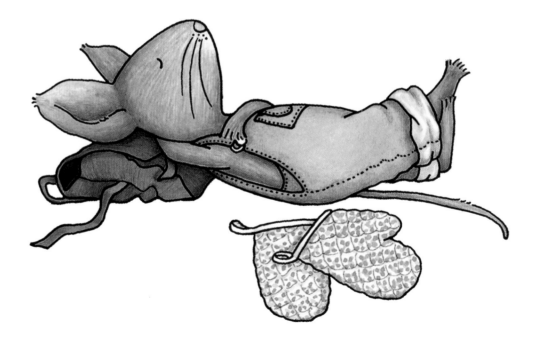

My Lunchbox

by Sarah Weeks

1. Shoes go with socks, Ba - gels go with lox, And
2. Boats go with docks, Paint - ers go with smocks, And

I go to school with my lunch - box. Ticks go with tocks,
I go to school with my lunch - box. Forts go with Knox,

Tow - ers go with clocks, And I go to school with my lunch - box. What-
Shep - herds go with flocks, And I go to school with my lunch - box. What-

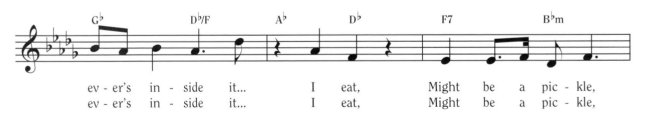

ev - er's in - side it... I eat, Might be a pic - kle,
ev - er's in - side it... I eat, Might be a pic - kle,

Might be some - thing sweet. I o - pen my mouth, Nice and
Might be some - thing sweet. I o - pen my mouth, Nice and

wide, _____ And down what - ev - er I find in - side.
wide, _____ And down what - ev - er I find in - side.

Sly goes with fox, Stub - born goes with ox, Hol - ly goes with hocks,

Chick - en goes with pox, And I go to school, to school, to school,

instrumental

I go to school _____ with my lunch - box.

Big Words

by Sarah Weeks

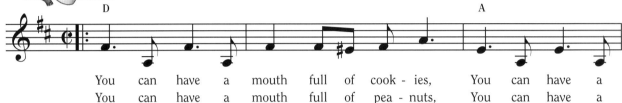

You can have a mouth full of cook - ies, You can have a
You can have a mouth full of pea - nuts, You can have a

mouth full of cheese, If you want a mouth full of big words,
mouth full of bread, If you want a mouth full of big words,

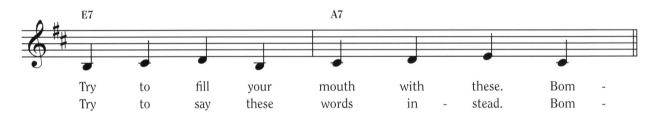

Try to fill your mouth with these. Bom -
Try to say these mouth words in - stead. Bom -

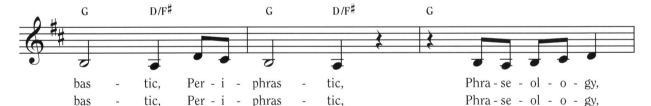

bas - tic, Per - i - phras - tic, Phra - se - ol - o - gy,
bas - tic, Per - i - phras - tic, Phra - se - ol - o - gy,

Et - y - mol - o - gy, Su - per - cil - i - ous, Per - spic - u - i - ty
Et - y - mol - o - gy, Su - per - cil - i - ous, Per - spic - u - i - ty

Or - a - tor - i - cal, In - ge - nu - i - ty, I love be - ing

Or - a - tor - i - cal, In - ge - nu - i - ty, I love be - ing

gran - di - ose And ver - y, ver - y ver - bal - ly

gran - di - ose And ver - y, ver - y ver - bal - ly

instrumental

ver - bose. Big words can say an aw - ful

ver - bose.

lot, But some - times_____ when you say them,_____ Your

tongue gets in a knot. Big words are some-times hard to

spell, But when you're say - ing some - thing big, They

sure do say it well. You can have a

mouth full of crack - ers, You can have a mouth full of pie,

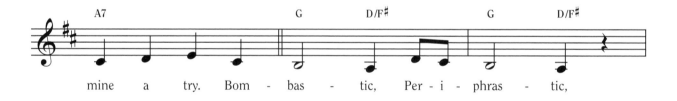

If you want a mouth full of big words, Give these words of

mine a try. Bom - bas - tic, Per - i - phras - tic,

Phra - se - ol - o - gy Et - y - mol - o - gy, Su - per - cil - i - ous,

Per - spic - u - i - ty, Or - a - tor - i - cal, In - ge - nu - i - ty,

214

G D/F# G D/F# G D/F# G F#7

I love be - ing gran - di - ose And ver - y, ver - y, ver - y, ver - y,

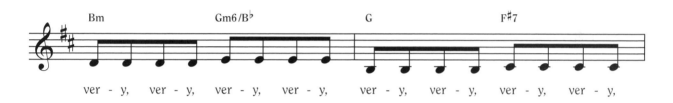

Bm Gm6/B♭ G F#7

ver - y, ver - y, ver - y, ver - y, Ver - y, ver - y, ver - y, ver - y,

Bm Gm6/B♭ G F#7

ver - y, ver - y, ver - y, ver - y, ver - y, ver - y, ver - y, ver - y,

Bm Gm6/B♭ D/A A D

ver - y, ver - y, ver - y, ver - y Ver - bal - ly ver - bose!

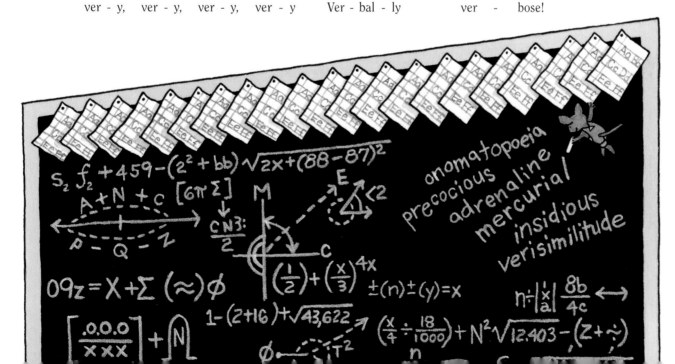

Explode a Messy Volcano

In *If You Take a Mouse to School*, Mouse makes a messy volcano that explodes all over! You can make a volcano explode too, but it's probably a good idea to put some towels under your volcano so it doesn't get as messy as Mouse's. Here's what you need:

1) An empty juice or water or soda bottle—this is going to be your volcano. (If you want to decorate it before you start the experiment, go right ahead! If you surround the bottle with playdough or clay, it will look very much like a volcano.)

2) Some baking soda

3) Some white vinegar

First pour about half a cup of baking soda into the bottle. Then, keeping your head away from the top of the bottle, start pouring the vinegar into the bottle until your volcano explodes!

So Many Mice!
So Much Popcorn!

In *If You Take a Mouse to School*, Mouse does a little math on the blackboard. Now you can have some fun with numbers and count how many pictures of Mouse are on this page. When you've finished, see if you can count the pieces of popcorn!

Mice: 16
Popcorn: 284

A Bedtime Story, Starring You!

In *If You Take a Mouse to School*, Mouse writes a book called *Goodnight Mouse*. You can write a goodnight book too, talking about what you and your family do at bedtime each night. Here's a fill-in-the-blanks bedtime story guide for you. Be sure to draw some pictures to go along with your story!

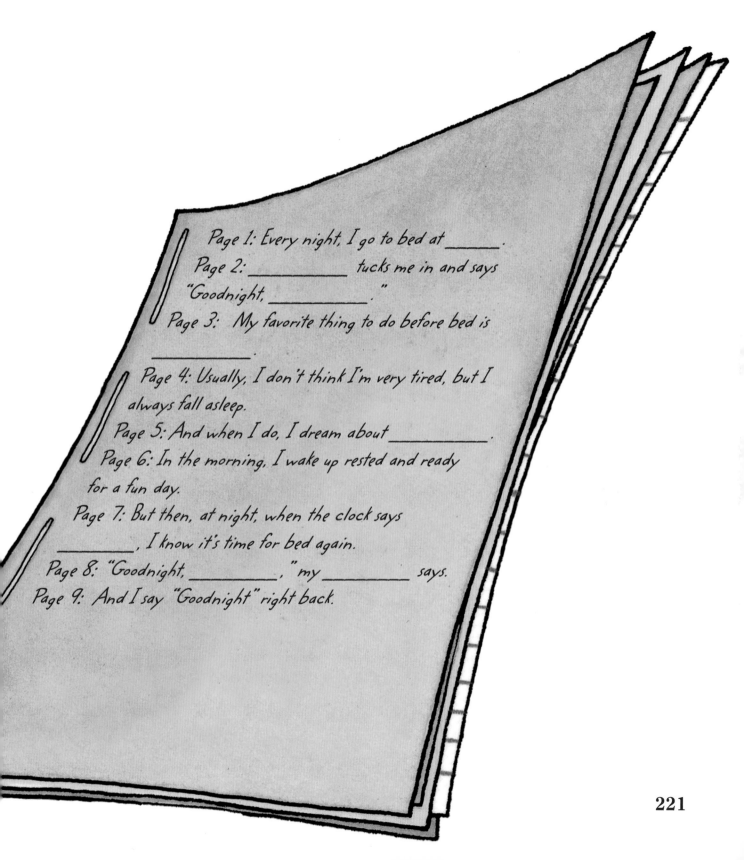

Page 1: Every night, I go to bed at _____.

Page 2: _____ tucks me in and says "Goodnight, _____."

Page 3: My favorite thing to do before bed is _____.

Page 4: Usually, I don't think I'm very tired, but I always fall asleep.

Page 5: And when I do, I dream about _____.

Page 6: In the morning, I wake up rested and ready for a fun day.

Page 7: But then, at night, when the clock says _____, I know it's time for bed again.

Page 8: "Goodnight, _____," my _____ says.

Page 9: And I say "Goodnight" right back.

221

Outtakes: From Felicia Bond's Sketchbook

boxer short underwear

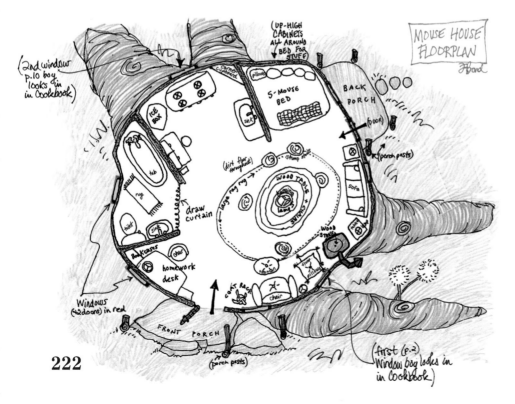

(2nd window p.10 boy looks in in Cookbook)

(UP-HIGH CABINETS ALL AROUND BED FOR STUFF)

S-MOUSE BED

BACK PORCH

MOUSE HOUSE FLOORPLAN

ICE BOX

(dirt floor throughout)

large rag rug

WOOD TABLE

draw curtain

sink

bookcases

homework desk

COAT RACK

chair

FRONT PORCH

(porch posts)

Windows (+ doors) in red

(first (p.2) Window boy looks in in Cookbook)

WOOD STOVE

(back porch posts)

(door)

sofa

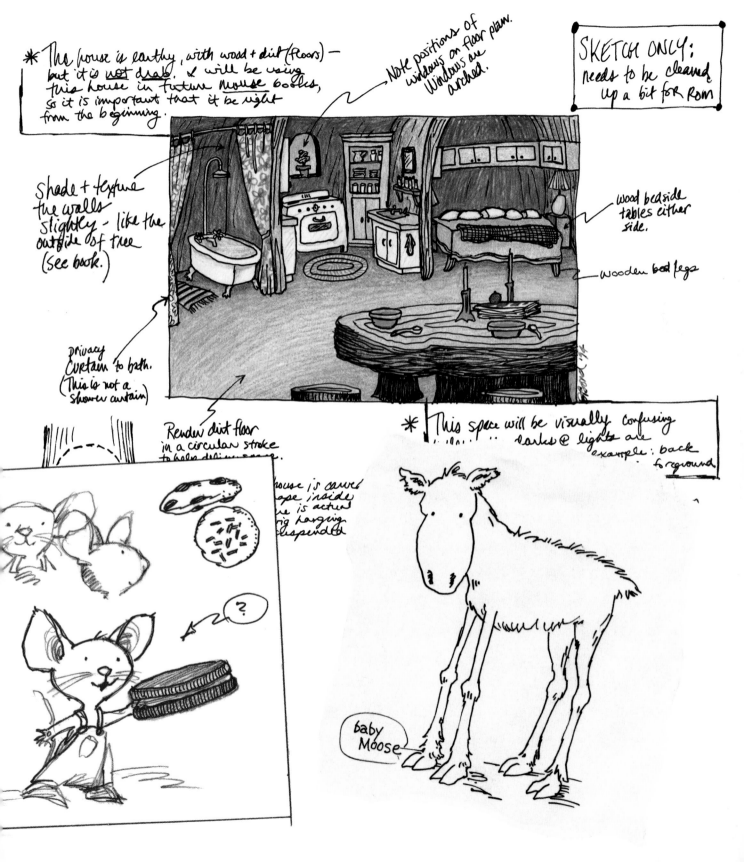

* The house is earthy, with wood + dirt (floors) — but it is not drab. I will be using this house in future Mouse books, so it is important that it be right from the beginning.

Note positions of windows on floor plan. Windows are arched.

SKETCH ONLY: needs to be cleaned up a bit for ROM

Shade + texture the walls slightly — like the outside of tree (see book.)

Wood bedside tables either side.

Wooden bed legs

Privacy Curtain to bath. (This is not a shower curtain)

Render dirt floor in a circular stroke to help define space.

...house is carved ...pe inside ...re is actual ...g hanging ...suspended

* This space will be visually confusing ...rks @ lights are example: back ...foreground

?

baby Moose

The End